When David was just a shepherd boy, long before he became a great king, his songs were known and loved by many people. Some, now called psalms, are still sung today. Shepherd boy, song writer, soldier, and finally wise ruler — here is the story of the king chosen by God to rule Israel three thousand years ago.

To Rachael
from Mrs Davison, June 1991
for attending Scripture Union

Acknowledgment
The illustration on the endpapers is by David Palmer.

KING DAVID

by JOHN PURVES LL B
illustrated by MARTIN REINER

Ladybird Books Loughborough

KING DAVID

Three thousand years ago there lived a young shepherd boy in Israel. He was called David, and he had seven big brothers!

David's father, Jesse, was quite a rich farmer and he owned lots of fields. His sons – David's brothers – worked in the fields.

Because David was the youngest brother, his job was to look after all the sheep. This meant that he had to lead his sheep to fields where the grass was green and tasty, and where there were cool streams nearby to drink from.

He also had to protect the sheep from wild animals.

The king of Israel at this time was Saul.

Saul had been chosen by God to be king, and had been appointed king by the prophet Samuel.

At first Saul was a good king, but he soon turned away from God and disobeyed Him.

In fact Saul disobeyed God so badly that God decided that Saul's family should no longer rule Israel. He would choose someone from another family to rule Israel when Saul died.

So God sent Samuel to Bethlehem to find a man called Jesse. When he had found this man, God would tell Samuel who was to be the next king.

When Samuel reached Bethlehem, all the leaders from the city came to meet him, because Samuel was well known and popular.

Amongst these men was Jesse, with seven of his sons.

As Samuel was speaking to Jesse, he caught sight of Eliab, David's oldest brother.

Eliab was tall, good-looking and strong, and Samuel thought, "That's the man!"

"No, he is not," said God. "You should not judge people on what they look like. What they really are may be quite different."

Six more of Jesse's sons also came. Samuel thought each one must be the king, but he was wrong. None of them was chosen.

"God must have made a mistake," thought Samuel.

But God had not made a mistake. He told Samuel to ask Jesse to call his last son from the fields.

When David came in, God told Samuel to "anoint him with oil", which meant that David would be the next king.

Life did not change much for David straight-away, and he was soon back looking after his sheep once more.

He often had to fight the lions and bears which attacked the sheep, but at other times when it was quiet, he would sit and play his harp and sing songs which he made up himself.

David's songs gradually became known all over the country, and we can still read many of them today in the Book of Psalms.

Meanwhile, as David sang his songs and looked after his sheep, at the palace King Saul grew more and more unhappy. No one could help him.

Some of the men in the palace told the king about David's songs, so Saul sent for David. He wanted him to come and live in the palace and sing for him, hoping that the songs would calm him down and make him feel happier.

David came to the palace as Saul had commanded, and his songs helped Saul to feel a little better.

While he was there David also found out more about what was going on in Israel.

The worst enemies of the Israelites were the Philistines, and they were getting their armies together to attack Israel.

Everyone knew that the Philistines spelt danger, and that when they began to build up their armies something had to be done – fast.

So Saul gathered the Israelite army and left to defend the country. David was not yet a soldier, so he returned to looking after his sheep.

Eventually the two armies met. The Philistines lined up along one hill and the Israelites lined up along another, with a valley between them.

Suddenly, as the soldiers were preparing for battle, a huge figure appeared from the Philistine army.

The figure was so large that at first the Israelites thought it was just a trick to frighten them. When they looked closer however they saw that it was no trick.

It was a giant soldier, nine feet tall – and that really did frighten them!

The giant's name was Goliath, and he challenged anyone from the Israelite army to fight him. But the Israelites were all too scared.

Even Saul, who was a strong and brave soldier, was terrified.

Every morning and every evening Goliath challenged the Israelites to fight and each time no one would come forward.

It so happened that one day David was sent by his father with some food for his three eldest brothers who were in the army.

As soon as he walked into the Israelite camp, David knew that there was something wrong.

David had just begun to talk to the officer in charge of the supplies when Goliath appeared once more to challenge the Israelites. He had been challenging them every day for six weeks now, but it still sent shivers down their spines.

But David was not afraid. "Who does this great boaster think he is?"

David's brothers scolded him for speaking like that, but Saul heard what he had said and called for David.

There and then David offered to fight Goliath himself, knowing that God would keep him safe.

At first Saul refused David's offer. "This man has been a soldier all his life, and you are only a child!" he said. But that didn't bother David.

"Your Majesty, back home I look after my father's sheep. If a lion, or a bear, carries off a lamb, I chase it and kill it. God has protected me from the lions and bears, and he will protect me from this Philistine."

At last Saul agreed. "But you must put on my armour first," he said.

Saul however was much bigger than David. His armour was far too big and heavy for David to wear.

"I can't fight wearing this," said David. "I'll have to go as I am."

So he took his staff and his sling, picked up five smooth stones from the stream, and walked out confidently to meet Goliath.

Saul could not bear to look, and Goliath began to laugh.

But although his enemy was much stronger and better armed than he was, David knew that God was on his side.

As Goliath strode proudly towards him, David took one of his stones, put it in his sling and fired.

Smack! It hit Goliath in the middle of his forehead and he fell to the ground. Immediately David ran over and cut off Goliath's head with the giant's own sword.

The Israelites went wild with delight. When the Philistines saw that their hero was dead, they all ran away and the Israelites chased them for miles and miles.

Saul was so pleased that he asked David to stay with him in the palace. While David was living there, Saul's son Jonathan became his best friend.

David became an officer in the army, and he succeeded in all the missions on which Saul sent him.

At first Saul thought this was good, but he soon became jealous of David.

For one thing, the people used to say that Saul was the bravest man in the country. Now however David was the hero of Israel, and Saul did not like it at all.

Saul was also worried that David would take his throne from him, although nothing was further from David's mind.

In fact Saul began to hate David so much that he wanted to kill him.

He always sent David to the most dangerous battles hoping that he would be killed. David however was successful in everything he did because God was with him and looked after him.

Saul became so angry with David that one day when David was playing his harp and singing to cheer him up, Saul suddenly flung his spear at David, and tried to pin him to the wall.

Luckily David saw it coming and moved quickly, but it was a close thing!

When he looked at the wall, there was the spear sticking out near where his head had been.

David pulled out the spear, but he did not throw it back at Saul as many people might have done. He just put it down, then went home.

When David reached home, his wife Michal, who was one of Saul's daughters, told him that he had better escape that very night. If he didn't, she was sure that he would be dead in the morning.

It was a good thing that she did warn him, because just as David was climbing out of the window, Saul's soldiers arrived at the door.

To give David a little more time to escape, Michal put a dummy figure in his bed and told the soldiers that he was ill.

The soldiers went to Saul for further orders, and when they came back to the house, David was quite a long way away.

Saul was angry and sent his soldiers after David.

Poor David had no idea of what he was supposed to have done wrong, because he had always been loyal and helpful to Saul.

He was so upset that he asked his friend

Jonathan to find out if it was true that Saul really wanted to kill him.

Jonathan came back with the sad news that Saul *did* want to kill him.

So now David had to escape. He was very unhappy as he said goodbye to Jonathan.

David set off to live in the mountains, taking some of his friends with him.

They had no food and no weapons, so the journey was a hard and dangerous one.

On the way they stopped at a temple and asked the priests to give them some food. The priests did not know that David was wanted by the king.

They also needed weapons. When they asked the priests, they said that the only weapon they had was – Goliath's sword!

David took the sword, looking at it thoughtfully. He remembered his battle with Goliath, and it gave him courage.

David and his men left the temple quickly, in case Saul found out that they were there. They went to live in a cave at a place called Adullam.

David was such a good leader that other people came to join him – poor people and some who were also trying to escape from the king.

David and his band of men had many adventures together and because they all trusted God, He kept them safe.

But Saul heard that David was hiding in the mountains, and he set out with his army.

David had chosen his hiding place well – there were so many caves that the king's soldiers could not find the men they were hunting.

One day however the soldiers came very close
to the place where they were hiding.

David's men must have been shaking with fear
when they heard somebody coming into their
cave.

Imagine their surprise when King Saul came
in!

He had left his soldiers and wandered into the
cave alone.

What a chance! David's enemy had walked into his hands.

"Kill him now while you have a chance," urged his men. But David refused to kill Saul.

God had made Saul king, and even if he was now a bad king, David was not going to take the law into his own hands.

He went up behind Saul very quietly and cut off a piece of his cloak. Then as Saul went out of the cave, David called out, "Your Majesty, it is me, David."

Saul turned and saw the piece of his cloak in David's hand.

"I am still loyal to you," shouted David. "You have no need to hate me."

Saul realised that David could have killed him, and also that David was a better man than he was.

He knew deep in his heart that one day David would be king, instead of his own son.

But none of these things made Saul hate David any less.

David had to face many other dangers, and had many more adventures before there was another great war between the Philistines and the Israelites.

When the Philistines invaded Israel, Saul had to give up his hunt for David at last. The Philistine and Israelite armies finally met at Mount Gilboa.

The battle was fierce, and the Israelite army was badly defeated.

When the Israelites knew that they were losing, they began to run away, but the Philistines caught up with them. Saul and three of his sons were killed.

A few days later a man came to the city where David now lived to tell him about the battle and the death of Saul and his sons.

David was very sad – sad to hear of Saul's death, in spite of what Saul had done to him, but even more sad that his best friend Jonathan was dead.

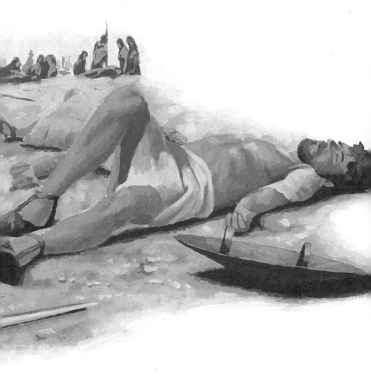

After Saul and his sons were killed, David became king – first of Judah, and then of the whole of Israel. He was a good and wise king and he reigned for many years.

When he was king he made mistakes just as everyone does, but he always remembered the greatest lesson that he ever learnt: to trust God at all times.

When he was a shepherd boy, God protected him from lions and bears, then from Goliath and from Saul, and now God had made him king.

When David was first told that one day he would be king, he must have been very surprised – but now it had all come true!

Although he was now a king, David did not forget about God, nor did he stop writing his songs.

When we read David's Psalms today, we can think of the things that were happening to him as he wrote and sang his songs.

He began his life as a humble shepherd, and ended it as the Shepherd King – a king who cared for his people as a shepherd cares for his sheep.